American Folktales for the primary grades, full of action and humor, are about America's best known and most loved folklore characters. Told in true tall-tale manner, each story has a simple plot and colorful illustrations. These delightful books, sure to appeal to beginning readers everywhere, are ideal for individualized or independent reading in the classroom or library.

Pecos Bill
Finds a Horse

by Kathy Darling

illustrated by Lou Cunette

GARRARD PUBLISHING COMPANY
CHAMPAIGN, ILLINOIS

To Honey, with love

Library of Congress Cataloging in Publication Data

Darling, Kathy.
    Pecos Bill finds a horse.

    SUMMARY: In need of a mount, Pecos Bill tries a
wildcat and a bear, and finally teams up with a legendary
mustang.
    1. Pecos Bill (Legendary character) [1. Pecos Bill
(Legendary character) 2. Folklore—United States]
I. Cunette, Lou. II. Title.
PZ8.1.D24Pe   398.2′2′09764 [E]   79-12079
ISBN 0-8116-4047-7

Pecos Bill Finds a Horse

2059192

One day down in Cactus Canyon, Pecos Bill sat on a rock and took off his boots. He rubbed his sore feet.

"It's not much fun being the best cowboy in the world," he thought, "if you don't have a horse to ride."

On a high cliff a big cat screamed. Now, as you may know, mountain lions are mean critters. And this cat was as mean as they come. Pecos Bill pulled on his boots just in time to see the giant mountain lion leap right at him.

The cat's twelve-inch claws sparkled in the sunlight. Sparks flew from its white teeth as they clicked thin air instead of Bill's head. The desert dust rose in a cloud as that cat hit the ground.

"You missed, pussycat," laughed the cowboy. Pecos Bill wasn't a bit afraid of mountain lions.

That big cat sure was angry. Again it leaped at Bill. And again Bill stepped aside. Every time the cat jumped, Pecos Bill moved away from the sharp claws.

Then *Bill* leaped, and he didn't miss. He leaped right onto the cat's back.

"Yippee-i-ee! Ride 'em cowboy," he yelled.

The mountain lion jumped 30 feet straight off the ground.

"Show me how fast you can run," hollered the world's best cowboy. "Scat, cat!"

The animal turned somersaults in the air. It twisted and turned. It ran circles around the tallest cactus. But even its best tricks didn't make Pecos Bill fall off.

After awhile, Bill reached out and grabbed a 26-foot-long rattlesnake. He whipped the cat with the snake to make it jump higher.

While jumping 100 feet high, the

shouting man, the howling cat, and the rattling snake headed toward the ranch in a cloud of western dust.

Well, about that time the cowboys were heading home too.

"Yahoo!" shouted Bill as he rode into camp. "I'm a real cowboy now. I have something to ride. Everybody come and meet Scat, my cow cat!"

The cowboys took one look at the cat and ran the other way.

Scat didn't like being a cow cat. The cows didn't like it much either. They were so afraid that when Scat growled they all ran away—even the biggest bulls. At night, Pecos tied the cow cat to a big rock in the corral.

One night Scat found some large sticks of dynamite near that rock. They looked like delicious red bones to Scat. The cat bit a little piece off one stick. It tasted as good as it looked. Scat ate the whole pile of dynamite and settled down to sleep.

In the middle of the night, Scat
woke up with a terrible stomachache.
The cat made so much noise that the
horses out in the corral couldn't sleep.
Scat's screams were terrible. The cat
moaned and groaned. Finally one of the
sleepy horses kicked Scat.

Well, you guessed it. KABOOM! The dynamite exploded. Scat flew through the air upside down and landed in a cactus patch. The cover of the chuck wagon caught on fire and the barn fell down. Scat ran lickety-split across the desert toward the mountains and was never seen again.

Now Pecos needed something else to
ride. One morning during a sudden
storm, he tried to ride lightning. It was
fast, but it only went one way. Bill
could zoom across the sky, but sometimes he had to wait weeks for lightning that was going back toward the
ranch. Bill wasn't getting much cowboy

work done. So he went back to walking.

Well, along about that time, Bill was walking down a mountain path and thinking about his tired feet when a bear climbed out of a tree. This was the biggest bear Pecos had ever seen. He was big enough to ride!

Pecos Bill caught him and rode him
into camp. In no time at all, Bill had
trained that grizzly to be a cow bear.

Curly Joe, Bullets Smith, and the
other cowboys didn't like the bear. He
was so strong he knocked down fences
when he herded the cows. Bill's big
cow bear pushed over the bunkhouse

one night when he tripped in the dark.
And when he jumped in the water hole
to go swimming, a huge wave flooded
the chuck wagon.

"My cow bear is strong, all right,"
said Bill one night as he sat by the
fire drinking coffee. "But did you notice
how slow he is getting?"

Just then the cow bear gave a loud yawn before going to sleep.

The cowboys hoped that the cow bear would slow down to a complete stop. Sure enough, it seemed like their wish was coming true. The colder it got, the slower the bear got.

"That darned old cow bear wants to sleep *all* the time," Bill complained to Curly Joe.

"And when I yell 'Giddy-up Bear' he just yawns. I think he is going to go to sleep for the winter."

Now, as you probably know, bears hibernate all winter. And that is just what the cow bear did.

Once more Pecos did not have a ride. There was a lot of winter work on the ranch, and Bill had sore feet again.

Well, as it got close to roundup time, Pecos began to hear stories about a great white mustang. This giant horse ran so fast the cowboys said that it was hard to get a good look at him.

"I tried to rope him once," said Bronco Jones, "but he was so quick my lasso burned up when it got near him. He is one wild critter."

At first Pecos didn't believe that

such a horse could be real. But the more he heard about the big white mustang, the more he wanted to know for sure.

"I'm the world's best cowboy," Pecos thought, "but with a horse like that my job sure would be a lot easier. We would be the greatest horse and cowboy team in the West."

That night he dreamed about the beautiful white horse. In the morning he set out with a "Yip-yippee-yi-yea" to find the great white mustang.

He walked down into Cactus Canyon, across the desert, and up and down two mountains. Around noon his feet were getting sore, so it was a good thing that just then he found horse tracks. There, right in the middle of all the other tracks, were the biggest hoofprints Pecos had ever seen. They couldn't be anything but the white mustang's prints, for sure. After a fast look, Bill knew that there were 2,327 mares in the white mustang's herd. All the tracks led across the plains and toward the mountains.

Pecos Bill forgot all about his sore feet as he followed the tracks of the giant horse and the mares across the plains. It was hot when Bill reached the top of a hill and looked down into a green valley. Sure enough, there were the 2,327 mares he had been following.

They were eating the sweet grass. On
another hill, with his head high in the
air, was the great mustang.

Bill was surprised. The horse was
not white. He was pure gold except for
a white mane and tail, a white spot
between his eyes, and four white feet.

The cowboys who said he was white were wrong. That horse had run so fast they had not gotten a good look at him.

The mustang tossed his head in the air. He smelled danger. Pecos knew he'd better do something fast.

Bill took out his rope and threw it

all the way across the valley. The throw was perfect, and the rope dropped over the horse's neck.

"Yipieeee!" yelled Pecos. He had his horse.

But with a mighty toss of his head the mustang broke the rope as if it were string, and ran into the hills. Bill

took off after the mustang, running as
fast as he could. But that great horse
soon left him far behind. Pecos and his
sore feet were no match for a horse
that could run like the wind.

About that time, Pecos knew he
would need a better way to catch the

mustang. He sat down beside a water hole under a cliff. And sure enough, an idea came to him. He rounded up the mares and brought them to the water hole. As you may know, a mustang is sure to come back for his mares. And that's just what the giant horse did.

By the time the mustang showed up, Bill had hidden on the cliff. At just the right moment he leaped onto the horse's back. The horse stood still for a minute. Then he started to buck. At that moment Pecos Bill and the golden mustang invented "rodeo."

That first bucking contest was the greatest, the wildest, and the longest rodeo ever held. Pecos and the mustang ran all over the West kicking up piles of rocks and earth. These were later called the Rocky Mountains.

The golden horse did everything to throw Bill in the air. First the mustang did high diving. He tried spinwheeling, then sunfishing, and finally high flying. He tried everything he could think of, but Pecos Bill stayed on his back.

Pecos would be the first to say that it wasn't easy. It took all of his skill and most of his luck to stay on.

As the wild ride continued, Bill began to like the big horse. He knew the mustang would never give up, so he started talking in horse language. "I don't want to hurt you," began Bill. "I am the greatest cowboy in the world, and I need the greatest horse on earth to help me."

The mustang was so surprised to hear a man speak in horse language that he stopped bucking. He listened as Bill went on. For an hour the cowboy talked to the wild horse.

"I'm thirsty now," Bill finally said. "And I'll bet you are too. Let's go over to that river and have a drink."

Bill slid off the golden horse's back and walked to the water.

The mustang watched.

Without saddle, bridle, spurs, or whip, Pecos Bill had ridden him. The mustang knew it was impossible, and he wanted to know more about the man who could do the impossible.

Bill cupped his hands in the water. As he drank, the water level went down several inches. "Go ahead," Bill said. "Have a drink." The mustang was thirsty. He pushed his nose into the water and took a long drink. But he still didn't trust Bill.

The horse eyed the man, and as horses often do, said nothing. But Bill started to talk again.

"I have a lot of work to do," he explained, "and I need help. I can't go riding around on a sleepy old bear. I need help herding cows and you are the only one I know of that can do the job."

By now, the mustang was listening carefully.

"But that's not all," Bill went on. "I'm kind of alone. I want company. You're my size. I'm your size. And, if I guess right, you sometimes feel lonesome for a giant friend too."

It was the truth. The horse often felt lonely. With that, the big mustang moved closer to Bill.

"I'm going to get another drink," the cowboy said. "If you want to come along with me and be my partner, have a drink with me."

He turned to the river and took a drink of water. The river was like a mirror, and Pecos Bill could see the horse behind him. Soon, by golly, the

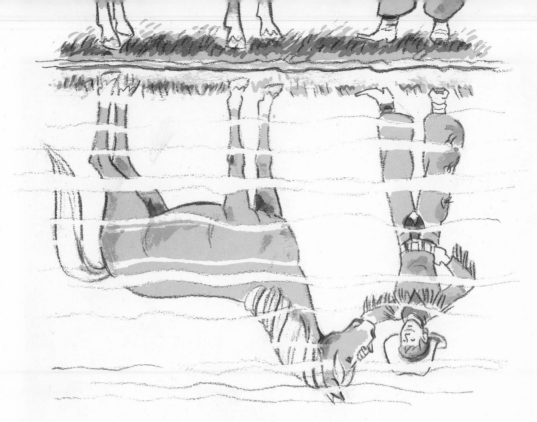

golden head bent down. Little waves circled out across the river as the great nose touched the water.

They were partners.

They drank to a new and wonderful friendship. They drank to the future of the wonderful West. They drank the river dry.